Even Me stirs a deep sense of faith and divine adventure in a young heart. Its much-needed message resists today's self-focused cultural narrative and encourages readers to look upward to God and then outward toward others. As a mother of sons, I'm grateful to Adie Camp for giving us a beautifully crafted book that tells the story of her own family's journey and inviting us to take one of our own. With clever rhyme and a razor-sharp message, Even Me will ready you and your children for a spiritual and practical quest worth taking. Read it yourself and then sit the little one you love on your lap and read it out loud all over again. You'll be so glad you did.

Priscilla Shirer
Bible teacher and author

Cover design by Juicebox Designs
Interior design by Left Coast Design

HARVEST KIDS is a trademark of The Hawkins Children's LLC. Harvest House Publishers, Inc., is the exclusive licensee of the trademark HARVEST KIDS.

Even Me

Text copyright © 2020 by Adrienne Camp
Artwork copyright © 2020 by Brit Cardarelli
Published by Harvest House Publishers
Eugene, Oregon 97408
www.harvesthousepublishers.com
ISBN 978-0-7369-7928-3 (hardcover)

Library of Congress Cataloging-in-Publication Control
Number: 2019016407

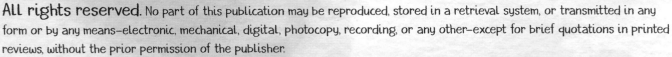

Printed in China

19 20 21 22 23 24 25 26 27 / LP / 10 9 8 7 6 5 4 3 2 1

HARVEST KIDS

HARVEST HOUSE PUBLISHERS
EUGENE, OREGON

Even Me

The ADVENTURE of TWO GIRLS REACHING OUT to SHARE GOD'S LOVE

artwork by
Brit Cardarelli

ADRIENNE CAMP with her daughters BELLA and ARIE

"Don't let anyone look down on you because you are young, but set an example for the believers in **speech**, in **conduct**, in **love**, in **faith**, and in **purity**."

1 Timothy 4:12

You're invited

There was
once an invitation
that brought excessive exhilaration.

A dream had been dreamed, and now could it be
this earnest desire would become a reality?

"We will need to raise funds..."
We wondered and doubted.
"Well, let's get to it..."
We jumped and we shouted.

We mopped, we cleaned, we babysat and sang.
We sold cookies, granola, butternut soup, and then
some friends supported and gave to our cause.
We counted, we added...now a round of applause!

We did it, we did it! We raised what we needed!
Now off to Uganda—our plans are proceeding!

We flew over
states, seas, countries,
and plains,
10,000 miles,
and that was just one way.
It dragged on for hours,
26 to be exact.

We were glad when we landed
with our luggage intact.

Even strangers were welcoming,
full of happiness and smiles.
It was a relief after traveling miles and miles.

We sat up in bed and looked at the clock.
It was three a.m.—oh my, what a shock!
Jet lag had us awake super early,
so sips of coffee kept us wired and squirrely.

Unsure
of how it
would all unfold,
feeling a little
nervous and
most certainly
not bold,

we prayed for our day,
trusting God to show the way,

Do Not fear I am with you, do not be DISMAYED, for I am your God I will strengthen and help you. I Will uphold you with my righteous right hand

Isaiah 41:10

and thanked Him for helping us see,
despite our weakness, He could use even me!

We sailed a
wooden boat to
a **medical island.**
Along with the locals,
we **stayed there**
awhile and...

made many things to help them survive.

Their life is so different, so hard and deprived.

Our hearts were burdened to think of all they go through.
We take things for granted, having so much
while they have so few.

People less fortunate, but equally loved,
not a matter of race, but made in the image of God.

They have dreams of what they desire to be.
In many ways, they are a lot like me.

Doctors, lawyers, pastors, and such,
though opportunities are few, they hope for so much.

We visited a **market** to try something **new**, they served us a whole fish— **head, tail,** and **eyes—Eeeew!** While others took a bite and got their fill, we hoped we wouldn't end up with a **fin** or a **gill**.

ALL of a sudden it was time to go.

With a sigh of relief and a big smile to show....

we drove to a place
whose name we're thrilled to know,
a lively small village called **Watoto**.
The kids stole our hearts, always curious and sweet,
full of wonderful songs and rhythm and beat.

We played

African drums

and sang songs together.
One day we'll be side by side in heaven forever.

Their faith was inspiring, so simple so clear.

They sang to their Shepherd—He's so very near.

we realized there's a void,
a job incomplete.

Our hearts were stirred,
although bittersweet

understanding God's love
can be found everywhere.

We were sad to leave
but eager to share,

You're never too young; don't
doubt that you're needed.
Don't ever quit—
trust the One who defeated
our fears and our doubt,
all the cares of this world,
to go to the ones who
will hear if they're told.

Share
His
word

Even Me

Whether you are heard
by many or by few,
sharing God's message
is the best thing to do.
Tell of what He has
done for your soul,
how He's given you life
and made you whole.

It doesn't matter your skin color, whether you're big or you're small.

We have a voice to speak loud, so let's make the call.

To share God's love with each other,

to be
**Christ's
Light**
to the world—

it's our joy to share Jesus, and for that cause we are sold.

Hungry Souls

by Bella Camp, age 12

The ground was lush,
the people kind
Great big hearts are what we find.
Hungry souls wanting more.
They need to know the gift in store.
No one spoke, so no one heard
about the wonders of God's Word.
We need to go, we need to say
that Jesus is the life, the way.
We'll have to go through thick and thin,
but think of what
in heaven we'll win!

AS we have traveled and **ministered** around the world, our family has had many opportunities to be in situations where we were cultural and religious minorities. When I first took my kids into these situations, I thought deeply about the effect it would have on them. How could I encourage them not to be influenced by the things they saw around them and not to conform to them, but instead to be the ones to bring change, even at a very young age? The Lord reminded me that when we bring light into a dark room, the darkness dissipates. We have **the light of Jesus in us**, so wherever we go, we bring the change. We should be the influencers. We should make a difference.

I hope and pray as you read this to your children, it will spark thoughts of where they see themselves in this story. What countries do they dream about visiting? Whom might the Lord give them a burden to reach out to? What words will they pray as they seek the Lord's heart?

How incredible it will be when they realize God has a wonderful plan and purpose for their lives. I hope hope this book, as simple as it is, will inspire new conversations and prayers in your home.

Until every heart is aglow,

Adrienne